Defoe Abbott Marx Hardy Machiavelli Montaigne Haggard Chesterton Cooper Emerson Joyce Austen Hugo Eliot Grimm
Melville Carroll Christie Molière Schiller
Stoker Maupassant Byron
Wilde Engels
Garnett Einstein Fitzgerald Hawthorne Smith Kafka
Goethe Dostoyevsky Hall
Cotton Kipling Doyle Willis
Baum Henry Nietzsche
Leslie Dumas Flaubert Turgenev Balzac
Stockton Vatsyayana Crane
Burroughs Verne
Curtis Tocqueville Gogol Vinci
Homer Widger Tolstoy Whitman Busch
Darwin Thoreau Twain Scott Plato Harte
Potter Freud Zola Lawrence Dickens Burton Hesse
Kant Jowett Stevenson
London Descartes Cervantes Voltaire Cooke
Poe Aristotle Wells
Hale James Hastings Irving
Bunner Shakespeare Cooke
Richter Chekhov da Chambers Irving
Doré Dante Swift Shaw Wodehouse Benedict Alcott
Pushkin
Newton

 tredition®

tredition was established in 2006 by Sandra Latusseck and Soenke Schulz. Based in Hamburg, Germany, tredition offers publishing solutions to authors and publishing houses, combined with world-wide distribution of printed and digital book content. tredition is uniquely positioned to enable authors and publishing houses to create books on their own terms and without conventional manu-facturing risks.

For more information please visit: www.tredition.com

TREDITION CLASSICS

This book is part of the TREDITION CLASSICS series. The creators of this series are united by passion for literature and driven by the intention of making all public domain books available in printed format again - worldwide. Most TREDITION CLASSICS titles have been out of print and off the bookstore shelves for decades. At tredi-tion we believe that a great book never goes out of style and that its value is eternal. Several mostly non-profit literature projects pro-vide content to tredition. To support their good work, tredition donates a portion of the proceeds from each sold copy. As a reader of a TREDITION CLASSICS book, you support our mission to save many of the amazing works of world literature from oblivion. See all available books at www.tredition.com.

Project Gutenberg

The content for this book has been graciously provided by Project Gutenberg. Project Gutenberg is a non-profit organization founded by Michael Hart in 1971 at the University of Illinois. The mission of Project Gutenberg is simple: To encourage the creation and distribu-tion of eBooks. Project Gutenberg is the first and largest collection of public domain eBooks.

A Princess in Calico

Edith Ferguson Black

Imprint

This book is part of TREDITION CLASSICS

Author: Edith Ferguson Black
Cover design: Buchgut, Berlin – Germany

Publisher: tredition GmbH, Hamburg - Germany
ISBN: 978-3-8472-1267-6

www.tredition.com
www.tredition.de

A Princess in Calico
By
Edith Ferguson Black

Philadelphia

[7] *Chapter I*

Sleepy Hollow

She stood at her bedroom window before going downstairs to take up the burden of a new day. She was just seventeen, but they did not keep any account of anniversaries at Hickory Farm. The sun had given her a loving glance as he lifted his bright old face above the horizon, but her father was too busy and careworn to remember, and, since her mother had gone away, there was no one else. She had read of the birthdays of other girls, full of strange, sweet surprises, and tender thoughts — but those were girls with mothers. A smile like a stray beam of sunshine drifted over her troubled young face, at the [8] thought of the second Mrs Harding stopping for one instant in her round of ponderous toil to note the fact that one of her family had reached another milestone in life's journey. Certainly not on washing day, when every energy was absorbed in the elimination of impurity from her household linen, and life looked grotesque and hazy through clouds of soapy steam.

She heard her father now putting on the heavy pots of water, and then watched him cross the chip-yard to the barn. How bent and old he looked. Did he ever repent of his step? she wondered. Life could not be much to him any more than it was to her, and he had known her mother! Oh! why could he not have waited? She would soon have been old enough to keep house for him.

The minister had spoken the day before [9] of a heaven where people were, presumably, to find their height of enjoyment in an eternity of rest. She supposed that was the best of it. Old Mrs Goodenough was always sighing for rest, and Deacon Croaker prayed every week to be set free from the trials and tribulations of this present evil world, and brought into everlasting peace. An endless passivity seemed a dreary outlook to her active soul, which was sighing to plume its cramped wings, and soar among the endless possibilities of earth: it seemed strange that there should be no wonders to explore in heaven. Well, death was sure, anyway, and after all there was nothing in life — her life — but hard work, an ever-recurring round of the same thing. She thought she could have stood it better if there had been variety. Death was sure to come, sometime, but people lived [10] to be eighty, and she was so very young. Still, perhaps monotony might prove as fatal as heart failure. She thought it would with her—she was so terribly tired. Ever since she could remember she had looked out of this same window as the sun rose, and wondered if something would happen to her as it did to other girls, but the day went past in the same dull routine. So many plates to wash, and the darning basket seemed to grow larger each year, and the babies were so heavy. She had read somewhere that 'all earnest, pure, unselfish men who lived their lives well, helped to form the hero—God let none of them be wasted. A thousand unrecorded patriots helped to make Wellington.' It seemed to her Wellington had the best of it.

'Help me git dressed, P'liney,' demanded Lemuel, her youngest step-brother, [11] from his trundle bed. 'You're loiterin'. Why ain't you down helping mar? Mar'll be awful cross with you. She always is wash days. Hi! you'll git it!' and he endeavoured to suspend himself from a chair by his braces.

'Come and get your face washed, Lemuel. Now don't wiggle. You know you've got to say your prayers before you can go down.'

'Can't be bovvered,' retorted that worthy, as he squirmed into his jacket like an eel, and darted past her. 'I'm as hungry as Wobinson Crusoe, an' I'm goin' to tell mar how you're loiterin'.'

She followed him sadly. She had forgotten to say her own.

'Fifteen minutes late,' said Mrs Harding severely, as she entered the kitchen. 'You'll hev to be extry spry to make up. There's pertaters to be fried, an' the [12] children's lunches to put up, an' John Alexander's lost his jography—I believe that boy'd lose his head if it twarn't glued to his shoulders. There's a button off Stephen's collar, an' Susan Ann wants her hair curled, an' Polly's frettin' to be taken up. It beats me how that child does fret—I believe I'll put her to sleep with you after this—I'm that beat out I can hardly stand.'

'Here, Leander, go and call your father, or you'll be late for school again, an' your teacher'll be sending in more complaints. 'Bout all them teachers is good for anyway—settin' like ladies twiddling at the leaves of a book, an' thinkin' themselves somethin' fine because

8

they know a few words of Latin, an' can figure with an x. Algebry is all very fine in its way, but I guess plain arithmetic is good enough for most folks. It's all I was brought up on, [13] an' the multiplication table has kept me on a level with the majority.'

Pauline smiled to herself, as she cut generous slices of pumpkin pie to go with the doughnuts and bread and butter in the different dinner pails. That was just what tired her; being 'on a level with the majority.'

The long morning wore itself away. Pauline toiled bravely over the endless array of pinafores which the youthful Hardings managed to make unpresentable in a week.

'Monotony even in gingham!' she murmured; for Polly's were all of pink check, Lemuel's blue, and Leander's a dull brown.

'Saves sortin',' had been the brief response, when she had suggested varying the colours in order to cultivate the æsthetic instinct in the wearers.

[14] 'But, Mrs Harding,' she remonstrated, 'they say now that it is possible for even wall-paper to lower the moral tone of a child, and lead to crime — —'

Her step-mother turned on her a look of withering scorn.

'If your hifalutin' people mean to say that if I don't get papering to suit their notions, I will make my boys thieves an' liars, then it's well for us the walls is covered with sensible green paint that'll wash. To-morrow is killing time, an' next week we must try out the tallow. You can be as æsthetic as you're a mind to with the head-cheese and candles.'

Pauline never attempted after that to elevate the moral tone of her step-brothers.

Her father came in at supper-time with a letter. He handed it over to her as she sat beside him.

'It's from your uncle Robert, my dear, [15] in Boston. His folks think it's time they got to know their cousin.'

'Well, I hope they're not comin' trailin' down here with their city airs,' said Mrs Harding shortly. 'I've got enough people under my feet as it is.'

'You needn't worry, mother, I don't think Sleepy Hollow would suit Robert's family — they're pretty lively, I take it, and up with the times. They'd find us small potatoes not worth the hoeing.' He sighed as he spoke. Did he remember how Pauline's mother had drooped and died from this very dulness? Was he glad to have her child escape?

'Well, I don't see how there's any other way for them to get acquainted,' retorted his wife. 'Pawliney can't be spared to go trapesing up to Boston. Her head's as full of nonsense now as an egg is of meat, an' she wouldn't know [16] a broom from a clothes-wringer after she'd been philandering round a couple of months with people that are never satisfied unless they're peeking into something they can't understand.'

'But I guess we'll have to spare Pauline,' said Mr Harding. 'She has been a good girl, and she deserves a holiday.' He patted Pauline's hand kindly.

'Oh, of course!' sniffed Mrs Harding in high dudgeon; 'some folks must always have what they cry for. I can be kep' awake nights with the baby, and work like a slave in the day time, but that doesn't signify as long as Pawliney gets to her grand relations.'

'Well, well, wife,' said Mr Harding soothingly, 'things won't be as bad as you think for. You can get Martha Spriggs to help with the chores, and the children will soon be older. Young folks [17] must have a turn, you know, and I shall write to Robert to-night and tell him Pawliney will be along shortly — that is if you'd like to go, my dear?'

Pauline turned on him a face so radiant that he was satisfied, and the rest of the meal was taken in silence. Mrs Harding knew when her husband made up his mind about a thing she could not change him, so she said no more, but Pauline felt she was very angry.

As for herself, she seemed to walk on air. At last, after all these years, something had happened! She stepped about the dim kitchen exultantly. Could this be the same girl who had found life intolerable only two hours before? Now the Aladdin wand of kindly fortune had opened before her dazzled eyes a mine of golden possibilities. At last she would have a chance to breathe and live. She arranged [18] the common, heavy ware on the shelves with a strange sense of freedom. She would be done with dish-washing soon. She even found it in her heart to pity her step-mother, who was giving vent to her suppressed wrath in mighty strokes of her pudding-stick through a large bowl of buckwheat batter. She was not going to Boston.

When the chores were done, she caught up the fretful Polly and carried her upstairs, saying the magic name over softly to herself. She even found it easy to be patient with Lemuel as he put her through her nightly torture before he fell into the arms of Morpheus. She did not mind much if Polly was wakeful—she knew she should never close her eyes all night. The soft spring air floated in through the open window, and she heard the birds twitter and the frogs peep: she [19] heard Abraham Lincoln, the old horse that she used to ride to water before she grew big enough to work, whinney over his hay; and Goliath, the young giant that had come to take his place in the farm work, answer him sonorously: the dog barked lazily as a nighthawk swept by, and in the distant hen-yard she heard a rooster crow. Her pity grew, until it rested like a benison upon all her humble friends, for they must remain in Sleepy Hollow, and she was going away.

Back to contents

[20] *Chapter II*

A Ten-Dollar Bill

'I suppose you'll be wanting some finery, little girl,' said Mr Harding the next morning as he pushed away his chair from the breakfast table. 'Dress is the first consideration, isn't it, with women?'

'I don't know about the finery, father,' and Pauline laughed a little. 'I expect I shall be satisfied with the essentials.'

Mr Harding crossed the room to an old-fashioned secretary which stood in one corner. Coming back, he held out to her a ten-dollar bill. 'Will this answer? Money is terrible tight just now, and the mortgage falls due next week. It's hard work keeping the wolf away these dull times.'

[21] Pauline forced her lips to form a 'Thank you,' as she put the bank-note in her pocket, and then began silently to clear the table, her thoughts in a tumultuous whirl. Ten dollars! Her father's hired man received a dollar a day. She had been working hard for years, and had received nothing but the barest necessaries in the way of clothing, purchased under Mrs Harding's economical eye. When Martha Spriggs came to take her place she would have her regular wages. Were hired helpers the only ones whose labour was deemed worthy of reward? Dresses and hats and boots and gloves. Absolute essentials with a vengeance, and ten dollars to cover the whole!

'You can have Abraham Lincoln and the spring waggon this afternoon, if you want to go to the village for your gewgaws.'

[22] 'Very well, father.'

'I don't suppose you'll rest easy till you've made the dollars fly. That's the way with girls, eh? As long as they can have a lot of flimsy laces and ribbons and flowers they're as happy as birds. Well, well, young folks must have their fling, I suppose. I hope you'll enjoy your shopping, my dear,' and Mr Harding started for the barn, serene in the consciousness that he had made his daughter happy in the ability to purchase an unlimited supply of the unnecessary things which girls delight in.

'You are a grateful piece, I must say!' remarked her step-mother, as she administered some catnip tea to the whining Polly. 'I haven't seen the colour of a ten-dollar bill in as many years, and you put it in your pocket as cool as a cucumber, and go about looking as glum as a herring. [23] Who's going to do the clothes, I'd like to know? I can't lay this child out of my arms for a minute. I believe she's sickening for a fever, and then perhaps your fine relations won't be so anxious to see you coming. For my part, I wouldn't be in such a hurry to knuckle to people who waited seventeen years to find whether I was in the land of the living before they said, "How d'ye do." But then I always was proud-spirited. I despise meachin' folks.'

'I guess I can get most of the ironing done this morning, if you'll see to the dinner,' said Pauline, as she put the irons on the stove and went into another room for the heavy basket of folded clothes.

Dresses and hats and boots and gloves! The words kept recurring to her inner consciousness with a persistent regularity. She wondered what girls felt like who [24] could buy what they did not need. She thought it must be like Heaven, but not Deacon Croaker's kind; that looked less attractive than ever this morning.

As she passed Mrs Harding's chair Polly put up her hands to be taken, but her mother caught her back.

'No, no, Pawliney hasn't got any more use for plain folks, Polly. She's going to do herself proud shoppin', so she can go to Boston and strut about like a frilled peacock. You'll have to be satisfied with your mother, Polly; Pawliney doesn't care anything about you now.'

Pauline laughed bitterly to herself.

'A frilled peacock, with a ten-dollar outfit!'

She began the interminable pinafores. The sun swept up the horizon and laughed at her so broadly through the open [25] window that her cheeks grew flushed and uncomfortable.

Lemuel burst into the room in riotous distress with a bruised knee, the result of his attempt to imitate the Prodigal Son, which had ended in an ignominious head-over-heels tumble into the midst of his swinish friends. This caused a delay, for he had to be hurried out to the back stoop and divested of garments as odorous, if not as ragged, as those of his prototype. Then he must be immersed in a hot bath, his knee bound up, reclothed in a fresh suit, and comforted with bread and molasses.

She toiled wearily on. The room grew almost unbearable as her step-mother made up the fire preparatory to cooking the noontide meal, and Polly wailed dismally from her cot. The youthful Prodigal appeared again in the doorway, his ready [26] tears had made miniature deltas over his molasses-begrimed countenance, his lower lip hung down in an impotent despair.

'What's the matter now, Lemuel?'

'I want my best shoes, an' a wing on my finger, an' the axe to kill the fatted calf.'

Would the basket never be empty? Her head began to throb, and she felt as if her body were an ache personified. The mingled odours of corned beef and cabbage issued from one of the pots and permeated the freshly ironed clothes. She drew a long, deep breath of disgust. At least in Boston she would be free from the horrors of 'boiled dinner.'

Her scanty wardrobe was finished at last, and she stood waiting for Abraham Lincoln and the spring waggon to carry her to the station. A strange tenderness towards her [27] old environment came over her, as she stood on the threshold of the great unknown. She looked lovingly at the cows, lazily chewing their cud in the sunshine; she felt sorry for her step-mother, as she strove to woo slumber to Polly's wakeful eyes with the same lullaby which had done duty for the whole six; she even found it in her heart to kiss Lemuel, who, with his ready talent for the unusual, was busily cramming mud paste into the seams of the little trunk which held her worldly all. She looked at it with contemptuous pity.

'You poor old thing! You'll feel as small as I shall among the saratogas and the style. Well, I'll be honest from the start and tell them that the only thing we're rich in is mortgages. I guess they'll know without the telling. I wonder if they'll be ashamed of me?'

Her father came and lifted the trunk [28] into the back of the waggon, and they started along the grass-bordered road to the station. He began recalling the city as he remembered it.

'You'll have to go to Bunker Hill, of course, and the Common, and be sure and look out for the statues, they're everywhere. Lincoln freeing the slaves — that's the best one to my thinking, and that's down in Cornhill, if I remember right. My, but that's a place! Mind you hold tight to your cousins. The streets, and the horses, and the people whirl round so, it's enough to make you lose your head. Well, well, I wouldn't mind going along with you to see the sights.'

He bought her ticket, and secured her a comfortable seat, then he said, 'God bless you,' and went away.

Pauline looked after him wonderingly. He had never said it to her before. [29] Perhaps it was a figure of speech which people reserved for travelling. She supposed there was always the danger of a possible accident. Ah! if they could only have started off together, as he said, and never gone back to Sleepy Hollow any more!

Back to contents

[30] *Chapter III*

Fairyland

To the day of her death Pauline never forgot the sense of satisfied delight with which she felt herself made a member of her uncle's household. Her three cousins—Gwendolyn, Russell, and Belle—had greeted her cordially as soon as the train drew up in a station which, for size and grandeur, surpassed her wildest dreams, and then escorted her between a bewildering panorama of flashing lights, brilliant shop windows, swiftly moving cars, and people in an endless stream to another depot, for her Uncle Robert resided in the suburbs.

They were waiting to welcome her at [31] the entrance of their lovely home, her Uncle Robert and his wife. With one swift, comprehensive glance she took it all in. The handsome house in its brilliant setting of lawns and trees, the wide verandah with its crimson Mount Washington rockers, luxurious hammocks, and low table covered with freshly-cut magazines, the pleasant-faced man who was her nearest of kin, and his graceful wife in a tea-gown of soft summer silk with rich lace about her throat and wrists, her cousins in their dainty muslins, and Russell in his fresh summer suit. Here, at least, were people who knew what it was to live!

'So we have really got our little country blossom transplanted,' said her uncle, as he kissed her warmly. 'I have so often begged your father to let you come to us before, but he always wrote that you could not be spared.'

[32] A hot flush burnt its way up over her cheeks and brow. And he had let her think all this time that they had not cared! Her own father! He might at least have trusted her!

She started, for her uncle was saying: —

'This is your Aunt Rutha, my dear,' and turned to be clasped in tender arms, and hear a sweet voice whisper the all-sufficient introduction: —

'I loved your mother.'

And then she had been taken upstairs by the lively Belle to refresh herself after her journey, and prepare for dinner, which had been delayed until her arrival.

The dinner itself was a revelation. The snowy table with its silver dishes and graceful centre-piece of hot-house blooms, the crystal sparkling in the rosy glow cast by silken-shaded, massively carved lamps, [33] the perfect, noiseless serving, and the bright conversation which flowed freely, little hindered by the different courses of soup and fish, and game and ices — conversation about things that were happening in the world which seemed to be growing larger every minute, apt allusions by Mr Davis, lively sallies by Belle, and quotations by Russell from authors who seemed to be household friends, so highly were they held in reverence.

Afterwards there had been music, Russell at the piano, and Gwendolyn and Belle with their violins, and she had sat upon the sofa by the gracious, new-found friend, who stroked her rough hand gently with her white jewelled fingers, and talked to her softly, in the pauses of the music, of what her mother was like as a girl. Verily, Aunt Rutha had [34] a wonderful way of making one feel at home.

She laughed to herself as the thought came to her. She felt more at home than she had ever done before in her life. She remembered reading somewhere that the children of men were often brought up under alien conditions, like ducklings brooded over by a mother hen, but as soon as a chance was given, they flew to their native element and the former things were as though they had not been. An inborn instinct of refinement made this new life immediately congenial. But — could she ever forget the weary conditions of Sleepy Hollow? She frequently heard in imagination the clatter of the dishes and the rough romping of the children as they noisily trooped to bed. Her nerves quivered as she listened to Mrs Harding shrilly droning the worn-out lullaby to [35] the sleepless Polly, and Lemuel demanding to have *Jack the Giant Killer* told to him six times in succession. It seemed to her the life, in its bare drudgery, had worn deep seams into her very soul, like country roads in spring-time, whose surface is torn apart in gaping wounds and unsightly ruts by heavy wheels and frost and rain.

She looked at her cousins with a feeling nearly akin to envy. Their lives had no contrasts. Always this beautiful comradeship with father and mother; and Aunt Rutha was so lovely—she stopped abruptly. She would not change mothers. No, no, she would be loyal, even in thought, to the pale, tired woman, whom she could remember kissing her passionately in the twilight, while bitter tears rained on her childish, upturned face. She would not let the demon of discontent [36] spoil her visit. She would put by and forget while she enjoyed this wonderful slice of pleasure that had come to her. There was just as much greed in her wanting happiness wholesale as in Lemuel's crying for the whole loaf of gingerbread; the only difference was in the measure of their capacity.

'What is it, dear?' asked Aunt Rutha, with an amused smile. 'You have been in the brownest of studies.'

She looked up at her brightly.

'I believe it was a briar tangle, Aunt Rutha, of the worst kind; but I shall see daylight soon, thank you.'

Mrs Davis laid her hand on her husband's arm.

'Your penknife, Robert. Our little girl here is tied up in a Gordian knot, and we must help to set her free.'

[37] Her uncle laughed as he opened the pearl-handled weapon.

'If good will can take the place of skill, I'll promise to cut no arteries.' Then he added more gravely, 'But you have nothing more to do with knots, my dear, of any kind. You belong to us now.'

They discussed her a little in kindly fashion after she had gone to her room for the night.

'The child has the air of a princess,' said Mrs Davis thoughtfully. 'She holds herself wonderfully, in spite of her rustic training, but I suppose blood always tells'; and she looked over at her husband with a smile.

'She has wonderful powers of adaptability, too,' said Gwendolyn. 'I watched her at dinner, and she never made a single slip, although I imagine there were several [38] things that were new to her beside the finger-glasses.'

'But she is intense, mamma!' and Belle heaved a sigh of mock despair. 'I don't believe she knows what laziness is, and I'm sure she will end by making me ashamed of myself. When I told her we had a three months' vacation, she never said, "How delightful!" as most girls would, but calmly inquired what I took up in the holidays, and when I groaned at the very thought of taking up anything, she said so seriously, "But you don't let your mind lie fallow for three whole months?" And then she sighed a little, and added, half to herself, "Some girls would give all the world for such a chance to read." I believe she is possessed with a perfect rage for the acquisition of knowledge, and when she goes to college will pass poor me with leaps and bounds, and carry [39] the hearts of all the professors in her train.'

'And did you see her,' said Gwendolyn, 'when I happened to mention that our church was always shut up in the summer because so many people were out of the city? She just turned those splendid eyes of hers on me until I actually felt my moral stature shrivelling, and asked, "What about the people in the city? don't they have to go on living?"'

'She is plucky, though,' said Russell admiringly. 'Did you notice when you were both screaming because one of our wheels caught in a street car rail, and the carriage nearly upset, how she never said a word, though she must have been frightened, for we were nearly over. I like a girl that has grit enough to hold her tongue.'

[40] 'She is a dear child,' said Mr Davis, 'and she has her mother's eyes.'

Upstairs, in her blue-draped chamber, Pauline spoke her verdict to herself.

'They are all splendid, and I'm a good deal prouder of my relations than they can be of me. I'm a regular woodpecker among birds of paradise. I wish I hadn't to be so dreadfully plain. Well, I'll ring true if I *am* homely, and character is more than clothes, anyway.'

She undressed slowly, her æsthetic eyes revelling in all the dainty appointments of the room which was to be her very own. Then she knelt by the broad, low window-seat, and said her prayers, looking away to the stars, which glowed red, and green, and yellow, in the soft summer sky, and then, in a great hush of delight, she lay down between the [41] delicately-perfumed sheets, and gave herself up to the enjoyment of the present which God had given her. She would not think of Sleepy Hollow. She had put it by.

Back to contents

[42] *Chapter IV*

A New World

Belle entered Pauline's room to find her cousin revelling in the exquisite pathos of Whittier's *Snowbound* before dressing for dinner.

The problem of clothes had been solved by Aunt Rutha in her pleasant, tactful way.

'You are just Belle's age, my dear,' she had said the day after Pauline's arrival, as she lifted a delicately pencilled muslin from a large parcel which had been brought in from White's, and laid it against her fresh young cheek.

[43] 'That is very becoming, don't you think so, Gwen? It is such a delight for me to have two daughters to shop for. I have always had a craze to buy doubles of everything, but Gwendolyn was so much older, I could never indulge myself. There is no need to say anything, dearie,' and she kissed away the remonstrance that was forming on Pauline's lips. 'You belong to us now, you know, and your uncle thinks he owes your mother more than he can ever hope to repay.'

Then she led her to the lounge which Gwendolyn was piling high with delicately embroidered and ruffled underwear.

'I did not know whether you would like your sets to be of different patterns or not, but Belle has such a horror of having any two alike that I ventured to think that your tastes would agree. The girls are going in town to-morrow to [44] order their summer hats, so you can finish the rest of your shopping then, if you like, and get an idea of our city.'

And then had followed a morning such as she had never dreamed of. The excitement of driving to the station in the exhilarating morning air, past houses which, like her uncle's, seemed the abodes of luxurious ease. Before many of them carriages were waiting, and through the open doors she caught glimpses of white-capped servants and coloured nurses carrying babies in long robes of lawn and lace. A vision of Polly in her pink checked gingham flashed before her. How could life be so different?

The ride in the cars was delightful, past a succession of elegant houses and beautifully laid out grounds, until she began to feel she had reached a new [45] world where care was an unknown quantity.

Then the city, with its delightful whirl of cars and horses and people. She had never imagined there could be so many in any one place before. She marvelled at the condescension of the gentlemen in the handsomely appointed shoe store, and blushed as one of them placed her foot on the rest. She looked in amazement at the elegantly furnished apartments of Madame Louise, and the wonderful structures of feathers and lace and ribbon, which the voluble saleswoman assured them were cheap at thirty dollars, and was lost in a rapturous delight, as, with the calmness of experienced shoppers, her cousins went from one department to another in White's and Hovey's, laying in a supply of airy nothings of which she did not even know the use; always being treated [46] by them with the same delicate consideration: there was nothing forced upon her, only, as they were getting things, she might as well be fitted too. Then to Huyler's for ices and macaroons, then up past St Paul's and the Common, and then home to a lunch of chicken salad and strawberries and frothed chocolate, in the cool dining-room, with its massive leather-covered chairs and potted plants and roses.

She was growing used now to the new order of things and smiled a welcome to Belle from the velvet lounging chair in which she,

Pauline Harding, who had never lounged in her life, was beginning to feel perfectly at home.

'What an inveterate bookworm you are, Paul,' and Belle looked at the pile of volumes Pauline had brought from the library to study in the long morning hours [47] which the force of a lifelong habit gave her, before the rest of the family were astir.

'You forget I am an ignoramus,' she answered quietly. 'I must do something to catch up.'

Belle shrugged her shoulders.

'What's the use? It is surprising with what an infinitesimal fraction of knowledge one can get through this old world.'

'Such a speech from a woman in this age is rank heresy!'

'Oh, of course, if you are going in for equal suffrage and anti-opium, and the rest, but I never aspired to the garment of either Lucy Stone or Frances Willard. I *do* pine to be an anatomist, and Professor Herschel says I have a decided talent for it too. However, papa is not progressive, at least he does not want his daughters to be, [48] although I tell him I might be a professor in Harvard some day, so there is nothing left for me but to fall into the ranks of the majority and do nothing.'

'Why so? Is there nothing in the world but suffrage, and opium and — anatomy?'

'Oh, dear, yes, there's philanthropy, but Gwen does that for the family. She is on every Society under the sun. Let me count them, if I can. There's the Society for the Prevention of Cruelty to Children, and the Society for the Improvement of the Moral Condition of Working Women, and the Society for the Betterment of the Sanitary Conditions of Tenement Houses. She's a member of the W.C.A., and the W.C.T.U., and the S.P.C.A.; she's on the Board of Lady Managers of the Newsboys' Home, and one of the Directors of the Industrial School for Girls. In fact she is [49] fairly torn asunder in her efforts to ameliorate the condition of the "submerged tenth."'

'"Submerged tenth,"' echoed Pauline wonderingly. 'Is any one submerged in Boston?'

'You dear stupid, of course! The unseen population in filth, rags and unrighteousness, and the rest of us in lazy self-indulgence, which, perhaps, in God's sight, is about as bad. I often think if each professing Christian took hold of one poor beggar and tried to elevate him, we should solve the problem a great deal sooner than by starting so many societies to improve them in the aggregate. I can theorize, you see, but the practice is beyond me.'

'But why don't you try it?' cried Pauline, her eyes sparkling. 'It is a splendid idea.'

[50] 'Bless you, my child, because it would involve work, and that is a thing I abhor.'

'But Gwendolyn must work on all these societies,' said Pauline.

Belle danced across the room, and seated herself on the arm of her chair.

'You dear old thing! You're as innocent as your own daisies, and it is a shame to take you from your mossy bed. Don't you know there is work and work? God says, "Go work in My vineyard," and we good Christians answer, "Yes, Lord, but let some one else go ahead and take out the stumps." The most of us like to do our spiritual farming on a western scale. It is pleasanter to drive a team of eight horses over cleared land than to grub out dockweed and thistles all alone in one corner.'

She leaned forward and began reading [51] the titles of the books Pauline had selected for her study.

'Homer's *Iliad* and *Plato*,—I told mamma you were intense— Hallam's *Middle Ages* and Macaulay's *History of England.* I had no idea you had monarchical tendencies. I must take you to our little chapel, and show you the communion service that belonged to Charles the Second, or perhaps it was one of the Georges, I'm not very clear on that point. My dear Paul, you're delicious! To think of anybody voluntarily undertaking to scrape acquaintance with all these dry-as-dust worthies, and in summertime!'

'It is not easy for you to understand how hungry I am,' said Pauline, with a tremor in her voice. 'You have been going to school all your life.'

'Unfortunately, yes!' sighed Belle. [52] 'But don't pine for the experience. You will soon have enough of it. May I inquire when you expect to find time for these exhilarating researches?'

Pauline laughed.

'Between the hours of five and eight A.M.'

'Horrible!'

She faced round upon her suddenly.

'I wonder what you think of us all? You are as demure as a field-mouse, but I know those big eyes of yours have taken our measures by this time. Come, let us have it, "the whole truth," you know. Don't be Ananias and keep back part of the price. "Oh, wad some power the giftie gie us, to see oorsels as ithers see us." I delight in revelations. Show me myself, Paul.'

Pauline hesitated for a moment, then she spoke out bravely.

[53] 'I love you all, dearly. You have been so kind! But, Belle, if I had your opportunities, I would make more of my life.'

Back to contents

[54] *Chapter V*

Pauline's Birthright

'Do you believe in altitudes?' It was Richard Everidge, Aunt Rutha's favourite nephew, who asked the question of Pauline, as they sat on the broad piazza after church waiting for lunch.

'How do you mean?'

'I mean that trilogy of exulting triumph over the trammels of circumstance that Mr Dunn gave us this morning. Don't you remember? "Life is what we make it—an anthem or a dirge, a psalm of hope or a lamentation of despair." Do you believe any one can live in such a rare atmosphere every day?'

'Of course she does,' and Belle laughed [55] merrily. 'Anyone who has courage to stroll through the Middle Ages with old Mr Hallam before sunrise, must have plenty of altitude in her composition. It is my belief she lives on Mount Shasta, in a moral sense, and I shouldn't be surprised to hear of her taking out a building permit at the North Pole, if she thought duty called her. But, Dick, how can you be such an atrocious sceptic as to doubt the possibility of one's living above the clouds when you know my lady!'

'Ah, but she is Tryphosa, the blessed.'

'Tryphosa!' echoed Pauline in a mystified tone.

'That is her name,' said Richard Everidge, with a tender reverence in his voice, 'and she deserves it, for she is among the aristocracy of the elect. I never see her without feeling envious, and yet she [56] has been a sufferer for years. I am amazed that Belle has let all this time pass without taking you to call at the threshold of the Palace Beautiful.'

'There have been so many other things,' said Belle, 'tennis, you know, and canoe practice and tandem parties.'

Her cousin laughed.

'But that is only when Russ and I are not reading up for exams. What do you find to occupy your leisure?'

'Leisure!' exclaimed Belle solemnly. 'Leisure, my dear boy, has been an unknown quantity ever since I undertook to pilot this most inexorable young woman among the antiquities of our venerable city. She is an inveterate relic-hunter; is enraptured with Bunker Hill and the Old South; delights in Cornhill, and wherever she can find a crooked old street that reminds her of Washington; [57] and pokes about all the old cemeteries, until I feel as eerie as Coleridge's ancient mariner. I believe she expects to come upon all the Pilgrim Fathers buried in one vault. But there is nothing special on the pro-gramme for to-day—we will go and see my lady this very after-noon.'

As they went in to lunch, Richard Everidge leaned over to Paul-ine and whispered: —

'You have not answered my question. Do you think it is possible for common, every-day Christians to live above the clouds?'

'If I were a Christian,' she said, in a low tone, 'I should want to get as high up as I could.'

When they reached Tryphosa's, they heard her singing. They waited, listening.

[58]

'Here brief is the sighing,
And brief is the crying,
For brief is the life!
The life there is endless,
The joy there is endless,
And ended the strife.

O country the fairest!
Our country the dearest,
We press toward thee!
O Sion the golden!
Our eyes are still holden,
Thy light till we see.

We know not, we know not,
All human words show not
The joys we may reach.
The mansions preparing,
The joys for our sharing,
The welcome for each.'

Then Belle opened the door softly and went in.

Pauline saw a large bay window opening into a tiny conservatory, which loving hands kept dowered with a profusion of [59] blooming plants. The room was large and dainty with delicate draperies, two or three fine pictures, and a beautiful representation in marble of the Angel of Patience, which stood on a buhl table, where the invalid's eyes could always rest upon it.

Tryphosa turned her head to greet them from the low couch, which was the battle-ground where she had wrestled with the angel of pain during years of physical agony. Her eyes were lustrous with a radiance not of earth, and a wealth of silver hair fell in soft curling waves about her face; her mouth, sweet and tender, parted in a smile of welcome as she held out her hands to the girls.

Belle caught them in her own, and kissed them gently.

'This is our cousin, my lady, Aunt Mildred's only child.'

[60] The thin hands drew Pauline's face down, and she was kissed on cheek and brow.

'Your mother was my friend, dear child, in the long ago.' Then she added softly, with her hands on the silver cross at her throat, 'Are you a princess? Do you belong to the King?'

Pauline shook her head, 'No, my lady.'

'I am very sorry.'

They sat down then beside her. She held Pauline's strong hand between her wasted fingers.

'Dear Mildred Davis! You have her eyes and brow, my child. It does me good to see you.'

'That is just like papa,' said Belle. 'He says he can almost fancy himself back in the old home with Aunt Mildred getting him ready for school.'

Pauline coloured with pleasure. No [61] one spoke of her mother at Sleepy Hollow.

She looked through the French windows into the conservatory.

'How beautiful the flowers are!'

'You love them? Of course you must, to be your mother's child. It is such a comfort to me to lie here and listen to them talk.'

'Talk!' exclaimed Pauline. 'Do they do that, my lady?'

Tryphosa smiled.

'Surely,' she said gently. '"Every flower has its story, and every butterfly's life is a poem."'

Belle broke the silence.

'We heard you singing, my lady; I do not think Pauline had thought you would have the heart to sing.'

A ripple of the sweetest laughter Pauline had ever heard fell through the quiet room, and Tryphosa's eyes flashed merrily.

[62] '"The pilgrims kept on their journey, and as they journeyed they sang,"' she said. 'Do you think there is anything to cry about when we are on our way to a palace, dear child? But Sunday is always my resting time,' she continued, 'I do not sing as much through the week as I should. I am tired often, and busy.'

'Busy,' echoed Pauline involuntarily, with a glance at the frail body propped up among the cushions.

Tryphosa gave another soft, merry laugh, and drew forward a rosewood writing-table, which was fitted to her couch.

'Here is where I do my work, when my hands are willing; and then there are my dear poor people, and my rich friends, and sometimes the latter need as much comforting as the former. Oh, there [63] is a great deal to do, dear child, for some have to be taught the way to the palace, and some have to be brought into audience with the King,' her voice hushed itself into a reverent whisper.

'And how about the pain, my lady?' asked Belle. Pauline's eyes were full of tears.

'Just right,' she answered brightly. 'Some days are set in minor key, and the Lord calls me where the waves run high; but so long as I am sure it is the Lord, what does it matter? Not one good thing has failed of all that He has promised, and soldiers do not mind a few sword thrusts when they are marching to victory. "This day the noise of battle, the next the victor's song." She closed her eyes and a triumphant smile played about her mouth.

[64] 'You seem so certain, my lady,' said Belle wistfully.

'Surely! "For we know that He hath prepared for us a city."'

'Now you mean heaven,' said Pauline impetuously. 'To me heaven is enveloped in fog.'

'It will not be, dear child, when the mists have rolled away, and in the clear light of the Sun of Righteousness you look across to the other shore.'

'Couldn't you tell me what it is like, my lady? You seem to know. I can't fathom it, and everything looks so dark.'

Tryphosa lifted a plain little book from a revolving bookcase of morocco-bound treasures, which stood within easy reach.

'I believe I will let Miss Warner answer you. "Would you like a heaven so small, so human, that mortal words could line it [65] out, and mortal wishes be its boundary? The things we look for are prepared by One whose thoughts are as far above our thoughts as the broad starlit heaven is above this little gaslit earth. And do you think that people are to be all massed in heaven, losing their various identities, their differing tastes, their separate natures? Going from this lower world so full of its adaptations, where colour and form take on a thousand changes, and life and pursuit can be varied almost at will, to a mere dead level of perfect felicity? To leave earth where no two things are alike, and go to heaven to find no two different! The Lord's preparations mean more than that. We should learn better from this lower world. No one pair of black eyes is just like another, no two leaves upon the same tree. And not a yellow blossom can spring up by the wayside, without a [66] red or a white one at hand for contrast. Are the clouds copies of each other? Are the shadows on the hills ever twice the same? Take for your comfort the full assurance that the very Tree of Life—which in Eden seems to have borne but one manner of fruit—in heaven shall bear twelve. But we cannot imagine it—in its fulness. We must look, not to see clear outlines and distinct colours, but only the flood of heavenly light. From point to point the promises pass on, with their golden touch; until the vacant places in our lives disappear, and the aches die out, and desire and longing are lost in 'more than heart could wish.'"'

A pause fell then, and a stillness, broken only by the plashing of a little fountain, whose drops fell among the flowers.

As they rose to go, Tryphosa drew [67] Pauline's face down until it touched her own.

'Dear child, won't you claim your birthright?'

'I will, my lady.'

Back to contents

Giving Oneself

The summer slipped away, and to Pauline it was a continual dream of pleasure. She adhered strictly to her habit of rising with the sun, and not the least enjoyable part of the morning was the three hours spent in the solitude of her uncle's luxurious library, while the day was new. Her active mind awoke from its enforced lethargy, and plumed itself for flight with a delightful sense of freedom. The dream of her life was coming true at last, and she was to have a chance to learn. She had learned all that the Sleepy Hollow school could teach her long ago. She would take up chemistry, of course, and [69] biology, mathematics and physics, French and Latin, geology and botany, and—well, she would decide later upon the rest of her curriculum. Her father seemed to take it for granted she should stay in Boston, her uncle called her his own little daughter, and she was content. Her healthy nature enjoyed to the full the innumerable diversions and pleasures which Belle's active brain was continually planning. Picnics and garden-parties, excursions to the beaches, where she was never tired of feasting her eyes on the glory of the waves; or a run into the city to hear some special attraction. Always brightness and fun and laughter, for Aunt Rutha's hospitable house was a favourite resort with many of the Harvard students, and it was the glorious summer time, when all the world—their little world—was free to be gay. She, [70] Pauline Harding, was like other girls at last!

Then she must learn to row and to ride, with Richard Everidge for her teacher. Belle taught her to swim, and Russell to play tennis, and Gwendolyn took her to some of the many meetings to which she devoted her life.

And then there was Tryphosa. She always made time for a visit there at least once every week. She was hungry to hear all she could about her mother. She began to understand how Richard Everidge, in the pride of his manly beauty, could find it in his heart to envy the woman who day and night kept close company with pain. Sometimes the shadows would lie purple under the brilliant eyes, and the thin fingers be tightly clenched in anguish, but the brave lips gave no sign. On such days Pauline could only sit beside her in [71] mute sorrow, or sing softly some of the hymns she loved.

'It is terrible to see you suffer so, my lady!' she cried, one morning, when, in the fulness of her strength, she had gone from the laughing sunshine into the shadowed room, where every ray of light fell like a blow upon the invalid's quivering nerves.

Tryphosa made answer with a smile.

'Not one stroke too much, dear child. It is my Father's hand upon the *tribulum*. He never makes mistakes.'

One day she slipped away directly after breakfast. She wanted to be sure of finding her alone.

It was one of the invalid's good days, and she greeted her with a bright smile of welcome.

'My lady,' she began abruptly, 'do you think I have forgotten all about my [72] promise? I could not. It has haunted me through everything, and—I gave myself to the King last night.'

Tryphosa's eyes glowed deep with pleasure.

'Thank God!' she exclaimed softly. Then she closed her eyes, and Pauline knew from her moving lips that she was talking with the Lord.

She touched Pauline gently.

'I had to talk a little about the good news with Jesus. He is my nearest neighbour, you know. And now, dear child, tell me all about it. What a wonderfully simple thing it is! People talk so much about being a Christian, when, after all, it is simply to be Christ's. We open the door where He has knocked so long, and let Him in. We give ourselves away to Jesus henceforth to live in Him, with Him, by Him, and for Him for ever. Dear child, [73] when you were giving, did you include your will?'

'My will?' echoed Pauline, startled.

'Why surely. The Christian is not to direct his Master.'

'But how do you mean, my lady?'

Tryphosa began to sing softly:—

'O, little bird, lie still
In thy low nest:
Thy part, to love My will:
My part — the rest.'

'That is His message to me. Yours will be different, for no two of His children get the same training.'

'I suppose now life will be all duty,' said Pauline, with a sigh.

Tryphosa smiled.

'That is not the way I read my Bible. Peter says we must "love the brethren," and John, "This is Christ's commandment, [74] that we believe and love," because "he who loveth knoweth God," and Paul, "The love of Christ constraineth us."'

'Well, but I must do something, my lady.'

'Don't fall into that snare, little one. It is what we are, not what we do. The dear Christ wants us, not for what we do for Him, but what He does for us. Listen: "He that abideth in Me and I in him, the same bringeth forth much fruit, for without Me ye can do nothing." "He that dwelleth in the secret place of the Most High shall abide under the shadow of the Almighty." The first great thing for you now is to "get your meaning."'

Pauline looked puzzled.

'I do not understand, my lady.'

'What are you going to stand for? How much better is the world to be for your [75] having lived in it? The day is long past when people were satisfied with a Sunday religion. True Christianity means a daily consecration of purpose. Look at the men who have made their mark in the world — reformers, inventors, discoverers, all men of a single purpose; and Paul says, "This one thing I do." Michael Angelo said, "Nothing makes the soul so pure, so religious, as the endeavour to create something perfect, for God is perfection, and whoever strives for it, strives for something that is God-like."

And remember, "perfect has no clipped edges, no dreary blanks." Little one, I want you to strive to be a perfect Christian.'

Pauline fell on her knees beside the couch, and buried her face in the cushions.

'I am not worthy,' she murmured.

Tryphosa laid her hand very tenderly [76] upon the bowed head, as she repeated in low, triumphant tones:—

'"I will greatly rejoice in the Lord, my soul shall be joyful in my God; for He hath clothed me with the garments of salvation, He hath covered me with the robe of righteousness, as a bridegroom decketh himself with ornaments, and as a bride adorneth herself with her jewels." "This is the will of God, even your sanctification." "That ye may be holy and without blame before Him in love." "Be ye perfect as My Father in heaven is perfect." According to the measure of our capacity, that is the idea, just as the tiny cup may be as full as the ocean. But for this we must lay all upon the altar. There must be no closed doors, no reserved corners in our hearts. We must give Christ the key to every room, so that He shall be, not merely a guest in the [77] guest-chamber, but the owner of the house. Are you ready for that, dear child?'

And Pauline answered humbly:—

'I want the very best God has to give me.'

Back to contents

[78] *Chapter VII*

A Great Surrender

The beautiful summer had slipped away and the glory of October was over the land. Pauline had crossed the borders and plunged, with all the zest of her thirsty soul, into the fair world of knowledge which lay stretched at her feet. Her three months of conscientious study had been of great service as a preparatory training, and already more than one of the professors had complimented her on her breadth of view, and the rapidity with which she was able to grasp an idea.

A subtle sense of power stole over her. Every part of her being seemed to expand In the congenial atmosphere. A brilliant [79] future seemed opening before her enraptured gaze. The world should be the better for her life. God had endowed her with gifts. She would lay them at His feet. She would devote herself to the uplifting of others. She would strive to lift them from the torpor of their common-place into a higher life. Life was magnificent! Poor Tryphosa, in her narrow sphere of pain, how could she be so happy!

Belle hurried along the hall and stopped at the door of the blue-draped chamber.

'My dear Paul, do you know we are all waiting? What have you been doing? If I could only get a snapshot at you now I should call it "The Intoxication of Success." You would make a splendid Jeanne d'Arc, with the light of high and holy purpose in her eyes; but as this is the last Saturday in the year that we shall have the chance of a ride to Forest Glen [80] and home by moonlight, I move that we postpone our rhapsodies until a more convenient season. The boys are waiting below with the horses, and the servants started long ago with the hampers. Even Gwen has been wooed by the beauty of the morning to accompany us, though I think there are about a dozen meetings on her calendar. Here is a letter for you, but you have no time to read it now.'

'Have I kept you? Oh, I am sorry!' and catching up her silver-mounted riding whip Pauline threw her habit over her arm, and ran down to where Richard Everidge held the handsome bay mare which had been her uncle's gift. The letter she had tossed lightly on the table. It was from her father, but it would keep. There was never any news at Sleepy Hollow.

Aunt Rutha watched the merry party as they cantered off.

[81] 'How well Pauline looks in the saddle. We have been very fortunate in our adopted daughter, Robert.'

'Yes, she is a sweet girl, and her passion for knowledge is just the incentive that our lazy little Belle needs. I only hope her father will never take it into his head to claim her again. She is a blessing in the house.'

On and on the riders travelled, through the exhilarating autumn air, until they stopped for lunch on the borders of a forest which Jack Frost had set ablaze, and which glowed in the sunshine with a dazzling splendour of crimson and bronze and gold. The hours flew by, and when they started homewards the sun was sinking in majestic glory, while on the opposite horizon the moon rose, silver clear. Pauline's every nerve quivered with delight. It was a perfect ending to a perfect day.

[82] When she went up to her room that night her eye fell on the forgotten letter. She opened it slowly with a smile on her lips. Suddenly the smile faded, and a cold chill crept into her heart.

'It has been such a happy day,' she had told Aunt Rutha, as, after the merry supper was over, she had stood by her side in the soft-lighted library. 'Such a happy day, without a flaw!' And now already it seemed to be fading into the dim, dim past! And yet it was only a few hours since Richard Everidge had climbed lightly up after the spray of brilliant leaves which she had admired, and she had pinned them against the dark background of her riding habit; even now they were before her on the table. She looked at them with a dull sense of pain.

'Mother has had a stroke of some sort, [83] ' Mr Harding wrote, 'the doctor doesn't seem to know rightly what. She is somewhat better, but she can't leave her bed. The children are well, except Polly, who seems weakly. The doctor thinks her spine has been hurt. Mother had her in her arms when she fell.'

Pauline shivered. Was this God's 'best' for her? The letter dropped from her hand, and she sat for hours motionless, her eyes taking in every detail of the pretty moonlit room, until it was indelibly engraved upon her memory.

When the morning came she took the letter to Tryphosa. She could not trust herself to tell the others yet.

The eyes that looked up at her from the open sheet were very tender.

'Dear child, are you satisfied?'

'With what, my lady?'

[84] 'With Christ, and the life He has planned for you?'

She hesitated. If it had been this other life that she had been planning for herself only the day before, how gladly she would have answered: but, if it should be Sleepy Hollow, could she say yes?

With her keen intuition, which had been sharpened by pain, Tryphosa divined her thought.

'I am going to give you a new beatitude,' she said, brightly. 'Blessed be drudgery, for it is the grey angel of success.'

'That is a hard gospel, my lady.'

'Perhaps, but ease and victory are for ever incompatible. The Father loved the Son, yet He surrendered Him to a life of toil, and Christ Himself gave His chosen ones the heritage of tribulation, crowned with the sweet, bright gift of peace. It [85] is the tried lives that ring the truest. The idea runs all through the Bible. "Silver purified seven times," and "gold tried in the fire," and "polished after the similitude of a palace." Have you ever thought of the friction that involves? The finest diamonds bear the most cutting, and it is the mission of the diamond to reflect the light. If we would have our lives a success, we must seek not happiness but harmony.'

'Harmony! With what, my lady?'

'The will of God, dear child. We are out of tune when God finds us. He puts us in tune with our great keynote Jesus, and then we are like an Æolian harp. The west and the east winds make music through it, and the shrieking storm the sweetest music of all. But remember, little one, it is the "joy of the Lord" which is our strength. We must sit in the sunshine if we would reflect the rainbow.'

[86] That night Pauline spent upon her knees.

'It is ridiculous,' exclaimed Mr Davis, when, the next morning, she announced her decision to the family. 'I will send a nurse down by the early train, but it is not fit work for you, my child, and besides we cannot spare you.'

Her eyes filled.

'It is so good of you to say that! But my Father has called me, and I must go.'

'He does not say anything about your going in the letter,' said Mr Davis, as he ran his eyes over the words.

'I mean my heavenly Father, Uncle Robert.' she said simply. 'The message came last night.'

After that they could not shake her, although Belle hung about her tearfully. Russell and Gwen protested, Aunt Rutha looked at her with sorrowful eyes, and Mr [87] Davis repeated that the very idea was absurd, as he paced up and down with a strange huskiness in his throat.

'I have come to say good-bye, my lady.'

Tryphosa looked wistfully at the brave, sweet face, which she knew she would see no more.

'So soon, dear child?'

'I have given Christ the key, as you said, and now I am under orders.'

'Well, I knew it would come. It is only that we must travel by different roads. We shall meet at the end of the journey.'

'But you never told me that my way to the kingdom lay through Sleepy Hollow!'

'Surely not, dear child! It is not for me to do the work of the Holy Spirit. I knew you would hear His voice speaking to you from out the shadows by-and-by.'

Pauline sighed.

[88] 'I have so longed for culture, my lady, and now I must put it by.'

'I am going to quote again. "Blessed be drudgery, the secret of all culture." Some one has said: "Latin and Greek, and music and art, and travel, are the decorations of life, but industry and perseverance, courage before difficulties, and cheer under straining burdens, self-control and self-denial are the indispensables. It is our daily task that mainly educates us, and the humblest woman may live

36

splendidly." And remember, dear child, a life like Christ's is the grandest thing in the world. Angels may well envy us the opportunity of living it, for God Himself has lived it in Christ and rejoices to live it again in each of us. We should glory in the thought that our King allows us to be the mirror in which the world may see Jesus. May the Lord keep you as one of [89] His "hidden ones," my darling, and make you to realise that He who "holdeth the height of the hills," spreads the hush of His presence over the valleys.'

Then she drew her close in a long, last farewell.

Back to contents

[90] *Chapter VIII*

Idealising the Real

'If you cannot realise your Ideal, you can at least idealise your Real.'

As the train slackened speed, Pauline lifted her eyes from the book which Richard Everidge had laid on the seat beside her, after giving her that last strong handshake, to see her father standing in front of the Sleepy Hollow Station. A great pity filled her heart—how worn and old he looked!

They had all wanted to accompany her part of the way, and Belle had pleaded to be allowed to go and help nurse, but she had said them nay. She knew the accommodations of Hickory Farm, and it was [91] easier to leave them where she had met them first, at the entrance of what would always be to her the city of delights.

Abraham Lincoln and the spring waggon! Had the whole beautiful summer been one delicious dream? Could it be only a week since she had stood entranced in that forest of flame? Here the leaves hung brown and shrivelled on the denuded branches, stray flakes of snow were in the air, and the early twilight fell chill and dreary.

'I'm terrible glad to see you, Pauline, though I hated to spoil your visit,' said Mr Harding, as he gave Abraham Lincoln a taste of the whip.

Pauline leaned towards him, and laid both hands upon his arm.

'Poor father! I am so sorry for you! Now tell me all about it.'

And the tired man turned to the daughter who for his sake had left ease and beauty [92] and friends, and shifted to her shoulders the burden which he found too heavy for his own.

The children crowded to meet her as she stumbled through the narrow hall-way into the kitchen. How dark it was! Her quick glance comprehended the whole scene, and the contrast between it and that other home-coming smote her with a keen sense of physical pain. She looked at the solitary lamp with its grotesquely hideous ornament of red flannel, at Susan's expressionless, freckled face, at the boys in their copper-toed boots and overalls, at the good-natured, but hopelessly common-place Martha Spriggs, with her thin hair drawn tight into a knob the size of a bullet, and her bare arms akimbo. 'Idealize her real!' Would it be possible to idealize anything at Sleepy Hollow?

She got her welcome in various fashions.

[93] 'It's about time you were getting back!' exclaimed Mrs Harding from the bed on which she was forced to lie, in bitterness of spirit, with Polly by her side. 'I suppose nothing less than a stroke would have brought you. It beats me how people can be such sponges! I'm thankful I was never one to go trailin' about the country after my relations. I never was away from home more than a day in my life till I was married, and it's been nothing but work ever since, and now to be laid here like a useless log, with everything going hotfoot to destruction! It's a good thing you've come at last, for the children are makin' sawdust and splinters of every bit of crockery in the house, and that Martha Spriggs has no more management than a settin' hen. I don't suppose you'll be much better, though. You never did hev much of a head, an' now you've been up among the [94] clouds so long, you'll be more like to sugar the butter and salt the pies than before.'

Pauline lifted Polly from her uncomfortable position with a warm glow about her heart, which all the sick woman's bitterness was powerless to quench. If she could see Richard Everidge, she would tell him that she did believe in altitudes now. It was possible even in the valleys to live above the clouds. 'Do not seek happiness,' Tryphosa had said, 'but harmony with God's will,' and God's will for her was Sleepy Hollow. 'It is not what we do, but what we are, dear child,' she seemed to hear her saying. She remembered reading that 'the smallest roadside pool has its water from heaven, and its gleam from the sun, and can hold the stars in its bosom, as well as the great ocean.' God could make a 'perfect Christian' even in Sleepy Hollow.

[95] 'I'm powerful glad ye've cum, Pawliney,' said Martha Spriggs, as she followed her into the dairy after the meal was over. 'I'm that beset I dunno where I'm standin', for Miss Hardin's been as crooked as a snake fence, an' as contrairy as a yearlin' colt, an' the childern dew train awful.'

'Yer've got to tell me stories all night, miles of 'em,' said Lemuel, as he bestowed his small person on the floor, with his legs in the air.

'No, no, Lemuel, you're going right to bed, like a good little brother, so Polly can get to sleep. Poor Polly is so tired,' and Pauline walked up and down the floor of her tiny room trying to soothe the weary child.

'Hi! Poll's no 'count; she's only a gurl. I ain't goin' ter sleep nuther. I'm goin' ter stay up fer hours an' hours, an' if yer don't keep right on tellin' stories quick, [96] I'll holler, an' that'll make mar mad, an' then she'll send par up with a stick ter beat me. I don't care, he don't hit ez hard as she duz, anyhow.'

'If you'll get undressed right away, Lemuel, I'll tell you about a little boy who lived with an' old, old man, and one night he couldn't sleep, but — —'

'Huh! that's a Bible story. This ain't Sunday. Par never reads the Bible 'cept Sunday. I want 'em 'bout lions an' tigers, an' men tumblin' down mountains, and boys gettin' eaten by bears.'

'What did you do when I was away, Lemuel?'

His lower lip protruded ominously.

'Ain't had nuthin'. Martha Spriggs don't hev any. She only knows "the cow that jumped over the moon," an' that's no good: 'tain't true, nuther, fer our cows don't do it.'

[97] No time the next morning for the long hours of delightful study. It was churning day, and there was baking to be done, and the mending was behindhand, and the children needed clothes; besides the numerous 'odd jobs' which Mrs Harding had deferred, but which she was prompt to require done as soon as she had some one besides Martha to call on. Then her meals must be given to her, and nothing tasted right, and the children were so noisy, and the older boys so uncouth.

Wearily Pauline toiled up the narrow stairs with Polly as the clock struck nine. She laid the sleeping child on her bed softly, so as not to wake Lemuel, and knelt down by the window. Not a sound broke the stillness. Her thoughts flew to the blue-draped chamber, and the soft lighted library, where she could almost see Uncle [98] Robert and Aunt Rutha, and Belle and Richard, and Russell and Gwen. But they might not be there yet; they had set apart this night, she remembered, to run over for a look through the big telescope. Last week that was, before she had decided to come to Sleepy Hollow, and broken up all their happy plans. Only last week! Then she thought of Tryphosa, lying with closed eyes in her darkened room, waiting patiently for the sleep which so often refused to come, while the angel of pain brooded over her pillow. Then her eyes sought the stars.

'You dear things!' she whispered. 'God put you in your places and told you to shine, and for all these hundreds of years you've just kept on shining. Oh! my lady, ask God to help me to make this dark place bright.'

She knelt on in the clear, cold moonlight [99] until at last the hush of God's peace crept into her heart, and there was a great calm.

The winter crept on steadily. Jack Frost threw photographs of fairyland upon the windows, and hung the roofs with fringes of crystal pendants, while the snowflakes piled themselves over the fences and made a shroud for the trees, and every day Pauline, with this strange peace in her heart, did her housework to the glory of God.

There were bright spots here and there, for the Boston letters came freely, and the magazines which she had liked best, and now and then a book, as Belle said, 'to keep Mr Hallam company.' They would not let her drop out of their life, these kind friends, and she took it all thankfully, though she could only glance at the magazines, and never opened the [100] books. There would be time by-and-by, she said to herself cheerfully. There was so much waiting for her in the beautiful by-and-by.

'It beats me,' said Mrs Harding fretfully, as Pauline hushed Polly to sleep, 'what you do to that child. I used to sing to her till my throat cracked, but you just smooth her hair awhile with those fingers of yours, and off she goes. I wish you'd come and smooth me off to sleep. I'm that tired lying here, I don't know what to do. That new doctor's no more good than his powders are. I don't see what old Dr Ross had to die for, just before I was goin' ter need him.' And the sick woman groaned.

Pauline laid Polly in her cot with a smile. This grudging praise was very sweet to her. To make darkness light, that was Christ's mission, and hers. [101] She was putting her whole soul in the effort.

'What makes P'liney so different?' queried Leander of Stephen and John, as they rested from their daily task of cutting wood. 'She used ter be as mad as hops if yer mussed up yer clothes, an' now she only laughs an' sez, "Never mind, if it's a stain that soap will conquer."'

'An' she's always singin' too,' said John thoughtfully; 'if mother didn't scold so it would be real pleasant.'

'I'd like to know why it is, though,' repeated Leander thoughtfully.

'Because she belongs to the King,' said the clear, sweet voice of his step-sister from the doorway, 'and she wants you all to belong to Him too.'

When she went back into the house, she found Lemuel brandishing a broomstick over the frightened Polly.

[102] 'Why, Lemuel, what are you doing?'

'I've casted the devils out of her,' exclaimed that youth triumphantly, 'an' they've gone inter the pig pen, whole leguns of 'em, an' they're kickin' orful!'

Back to contents

[103] *Chapter IX*

A Lost Letter

Seven years had gone by, and every day of each successive month had been full to overflowing of hard work for Pauline.

'Dear Tryphosa,' she whispered to herself with a smile, 'you little thought, when you gave me that new beatitude, what constant friends the grey angel of Drudgery and I were to be.'

She climbed slowly up the narrow stairs to her room, and shaded the lamp that it might not disturb Polly's troubled sleep,—poor Polly, who would be an invalid for life. Then she sat down with a sigh of relief to read Belle's last letter. It had been a hard day, her step-mother had been [104] more than usually restless, and the farm-work had been very heavy, for Martha Spriggs was home on a visit; every nerve in her body seemed to quiver with the strain.

'My dearest Paul,' Belle wrote, 'I can hardly see for crying, but I promised her that you should know at once.

'Tryphosa went away from us to "the other shore" last night. We were all there—her "inner circle" as she used to call us—all except you, and she seemed to miss you so. I never knew her to grow fond of any one in so short a time, but she took you right into her heart from the first. If I had not loved you so much I should have been jealous, but who could be jealous of you, you precious, brave saint?

'I have heard of the gate of heaven, but last night we were there.

[105] 'Dick was supporting her in his arms, poor Dick, he was so fond of her, and it was so hard for her to breathe—and we were all gathered round her, our hearts breaking to think it was the last time. She has suffered terribly lately, but at the last the pain left her, and she lay with the very rapture of heaven on her dear face, talking so brightly of how we should do after she had gone. It was just as if she were going on a pleasure trip, and we were to follow later. She turned to me with her lovely eyes all aglow with joy, and said:—

'"Give my Bible to the dear child in the valley" (that was what she always called you), "and tell her 'the miles to heaven are but short and few.'"

'She had a message for us all, and then, suddenly, just as the dawn broke, a great light swept over her face and she turned [106] her head and whispered, "Jesus!" just as if He were close beside her, and then — she was gone.

'I shall never forget it. I have always thought of Death as the King of Terrors, but last night it was the coming of the Bridegroom for His own.'

With a low cry Pauline's head dropped. There could never be anyone just like 'my lady,' and she had gone away.

The hours passed silently, as she sat benumbed in the grasp of her great sorrow.

Suddenly she sprang up. Her father was calling her from the foot of the stairs.

'Mother's had a bad turn. Send Stephen for the doctor, and come, quick!'

She hurried down, and mechanically heated water, and did what she could [107] to help the stricken woman, but before the doctor could reach the house, the Angel of Death had swept over the threshold, and Pauline and her father were left alone.

'Here's a letter for yer, Pawliney. Don't yer wish yer may git it?' and Lemuel, the irrepressible, waved it at her tantalisingly from the top of the tall hickory, where he had perched himself, like the monkey that he was.

She saw the Boston post-mark, and stretched out her hands for it longingly.

'Bring it down, there's a dear boy.'

'Not much! I bet Leander that I could make you mad, an' he bet his new jack-knife that I couldn't. I'm goin' to chew it up. It's orful thin, 'taint no good anyhow. You won't miss it, P'liney,' and crushing the letter into a [108] small wad he put it into his capacious mouth.

It was, as Lemuel said, 'awful thin,' not much like the volumes which Belle usually wrote. She had not been able to distinguish the writing, but, of course, it must be from Belle. The two cousins had grown very near to each other as the years rolled by, and a summer never passed without some of her uncle's family spending a week or two in Sleepy Hollow. Those were Pauline's red-letter days—the bright, scintillating points where she was brought into touch again with the world of thought and light and beauty.

'Throw it down to me, Lemuel, dear.'

'Can't,' said the boy coolly, 'I'm goin' ter tie it to Poll's balloon, an' let go of the string, an' then it'll go straight to heaven,' and, with the letter reposing in his cheek, he began to sing vociferously:—

[109]

> '"I want ter be an angel,
> An' with the angels stand;
> A crown upon my forehead,
> A harp within my hand."

'Git mad now, P'liney, quick, fer I want that knife orful.'

A cry from Polly made Pauline hurry into the house to find that Martha Spriggs had slipped while passing the child's couch, and upset a bowl of scalding milk, which she was carrying, right over the little invalid's foot. In the confusion which followed, Pauline forgot Lemuel and her longed-for letter. When she went out to look for him he was gone.

'Give it to me now, Lemuel,' she said, as he came into supper; 'you've had enough fun for to-day.'

'Can't P'liney. I used it fer a gun wad to shoot a squirrel with, an' the cat ate the squirrel, letter an' all. Yer [110] don't want me ter kill the cat, do yer, P'liney?'

'Oh! Lemuel,' she cried softly, 'how could you? How could you do it?'

44

She sighed sorrowfully. She had tried so hard to make Lemuel a good boy, but nothing seemed to touch him, and, young as he was, the neighbours had begun to lay the blame of every misdeed upon his shoulders, and Deacon Croaker predicted with a mournful shake of his head, 'No good will ever come of Lemuel Harding. He's a bad lot, a bad lot.'

'Sing to me!' cried Polly, 'the pain's awful!' and taking the weary little form in her arms, Pauline sang herself back into her usual happy trust.

She would not tell Belle her letter had been destroyed. She must shield Lemuel.

'I'm doing my best,' she said to herself, 'God understands.'

[111] 'Ain't yer mad yit?' whispered Lemuel anxiously, as he peered into the bright peaceful face on his way to bed.

The hand that stroked his tumbled hair was very gentle.

'No, Lemuel, only sorry that my boy forgot the King was looking on.'

With a shame-faced look the boy's hand sought his pocket, but Satan whispered, 'She may be mad to-morrow,' and he crept away.

'What are you teasing Pauline about?' asked Stephen, as he went upstairs.

'Ain't doin' nuthin',' was the sullen reply.

'Yes, you are. She don't hev sorrowful looks in her eyes unless you're cuttin' up worse than common. You've just got to leave off sudden, or I'll give you something you won't ever forgit.'

'Ain't goin' ter be bossed by nobody, [112] ' said the boy dogged-ly, as he reached his room. 'Was goin' ter give her the old letter to-morrow, anyway, but now I don't care if she never gits it,' and opening the chest which held his few treasures, he deliberately shut up the letter in an old tin box, and went to bed.

'Father is gettin' so mortal queer,' said Stephen discontentedly. 'First he tells me to top-dress the upper lot, and then right off he wants me to harness up and go to the mill. I don't see how a feller's to know what to do. Most wish I'd gone West with Leander, it's a free life there, and he's his own master.'

'"One is our Master, even Christ,"' Pauline quoted softly. 'Don't go, Stephen, you and Lemuel are the only ones on the farm now, and father is getting old.'

She spoke sadly. She had noticed with [113] a sinking heart how 'queer' her father was.

The years had slipped by until Polly was seventeen. A very frail little body she was, but always so patient and sweet, that Pauline never grudged the constant care.

Two of the boys had taken the shaping of their own lives and gone away, and Susan Ann had a home of her own with two little freckled-faced children to call her mother.

'We'll jog along together, Stephen,' she said in her bright, cheery way. 'Father forgets now and then, but he doesn't mean any harm, and it's only one day at a time, you know.'

Stephen looked at her admiringly.

'You're a brick, Pawliney, and I guess if you can stand it, I ought to be able to, with you round making the sunshine. I'd [114] be a brute to go and leave you and Lem with it all on your shoulders'; and the honest, good-hearted fellow went in to give Polly a kiss before he started for the mill.

Clearing out an old trunk next day Pauline came across a soiled, tumbled envelope. It was the letter which Lemuel had tucked away and forgotten while he waited for her to 'get mad.'

She opened it eagerly. It was from Richard Everidge.

'I should like to come down and see you,' he wrote, 'in Sleepy Hollow, that is, if you care to have me, and it is quite convenient. Do not trouble to write unless you want me. If I do not get an answer I shall know you do not care.'

Richard Everidge had been married for three years now, and had a little girl.

[115] She clasped her hands with one quick cry of pain. What must he have thought of her all these years? Her friend, who had always been so kind! so kind!

'Pawliney!' called her father, in the querulous accents of one whose brain is weakening. 'Pawliney, I wish you'd come down and sing a little, the house is terrible lonesome since mother's gone.'

And Pauline sang, in her full, sweet tones:—

> '"God moves in a mysterious way
> His wonders to perform."'

'God is good, Pawliney?'

'Yes, father.'

'He never makes mistakes?'

'Oh, no, father.'

'You believe that, Pawliney?'

'Yes, yes, I know it, father.'

[116] And her voice rang out triumphantly in another stanza:—

> '"Judge not the Lord by feeble sense,
> But trust Him for His grace:
> Behind a frowning providence
> He hides a smiling face."'

Back to contents

[117] *Chapter X*

The Angel of Patience

'Here's the mortgage money, Pawliney,' said Stephen, as he handed her a roll of bank-notes. 'It's not due for a month yet, but I'll be away for a week at the Bend, and if father gets hold of it he'll take it to make matches of, as like as not. You'd better stow it away somewheres till the time comes.'

'Very well, Stephen, I'll put it in my strong box, and carry the key in my pocket. You won't be away at the Bend any longer than you can help, Stephen? It's such a comfort to have you in the house.'

They were standing by the light waggon, [118] which Lemuel had brought round from the barn, ready for Stephen's journey.

'Don't know about the comfort part, Pawliney,' said Stephen, with a queer choke in his voice. 'Seems like as if we all depended on you for that commodity. But I'll be as quick as I kin. Good-bye, all of you. Git along, Goliath.'

Three days had passed since his departure, and Pauline stood in the doorway feasting her eyes on the lights and shadows which grouped themselves about the distant hills, when Lemuel brushed past her, clad in his Sunday best.

'Why, Lemuel!' she cried astonished, 'you haven't had your supper yet. Where are you going?'

'To China,' was the brusque response. 'I've hed enuff of Sleepy Hollow, an' bein' ordered round by an old man with his head in the moon. It's "Lemuel, do this," an' before [119] I git started it's "Lemuel, do the t'other thing." You kin stand it ef you're a mind ter; I won't.'

'But, Lemuel!' gasped Pauline, 'what will Stephen say?'

'I don't care what he says,' said the boy roughly. 'Stephen ain't my boss.'

'Oh, Lemuel, you can't mean it!' cried Pauline, as she followed him down the path to the main road.

'See if I don't!' And he strode away from her, and vaulted over the gate.

'But what will father do?'

'Git somebody that's ez loony ez himself. I ain't,' was the jeering reply.

'Lemuel, you mustn't go, it will kill father!' and Pauline stretched out her hands to him appealingly.

A mocking laugh was the only reply as he disappeared round a bend of the road.

[120] Pauline went slowly back to the house feeling bruised and stunned.

'Pawliney,' piped her father in his shrill voice, 'where's Lemuel? I told him to take the horse to the forge, and hoe the potatoes, and weed the onions, and go to the woods for a load. I don't see how I'm to get through with such a lot of heedless boys around. What hev you done with him? You just spoil them all with your cossetin'.'

'It will all come right, father,' said Pauline soothingly. 'Lemuel has gone away for awhile.'

'Away!' echoed the old man suspiciously. 'Away, Pawliney? Did you know he was going?'

'Yes, father; he will be back by-and-by, and Stephen will be home next week.'

She paced her room that night with a heavy heart. There was no way to hinder [121] the misguided boy. Before Stephen could follow him he would be on the sea. He had often declared he meant to be a sailor. Suddenly she stopped, thunder-struck. The lid of her strong box had been forced open! With an awful dread at her heart she lifted it and looked in. The money was gone!

With a bitter cry she fell upon her knees. 'A thief!' Her Lemuel. The boy that she had borne with and prayed over all these years! And the money was due in a month! What should she do? Stephen must never know—Stephen, with his stalwart honesty and upright soul. His anger would be terrible, and she must shield Lemuel all she could. Poor Lemuel!

All night long she pondered sorrowfully. When the morning came she went to Deacon Croaker.

[122] 'I hear you are behindhand with your wool,' she said, in her straightforward way. 'I will spin it for you if you like, and, Deacon, may I ask you as a favour to let me have the money in advance?'

The deacon looked at her curiously.

'Hard up, air ye, Pawliney? Well, well, don't colour up so, we all hev our scarce times. I ain't partial to payin' forehanded, but you was awful kind to Mis' Croaker when her rheumatiz was bad on her, an' I ain't one ter forgit a favour. Cum in, Pawliney, while I git the money. Mis' Croaker will be rale pleased; she thinks you're the best spinner in the valley.'

'No, thank you, I will wait out here.'

The old man hobbled into the house, and she stood waiting, clothed in her sorrow and shame.

'So Lemuel's ben an' tuk French [123] leave?' he said, as he handed her the money. 'Well, well, I allers did say that boy'd be a heart break tew ye, Pawliney. Well, what's gone's forgot. Don't fret over him, Pawliney, he was a bad lot, a bad lot. Ye'er well rid of him, my dear.'

'I never shall forget him,' Pauline said gravely, 'and he can't get away from God, Deacon Croaker.'

She counted the bills as she hurried along. It would just make enough, with the butter money. That was all she had for clothes for herself and Polly—but Polly had enough for a while, and she could go without.

In the evenings, long after the others were in bed, she paced up and down the kitchen, spinning Deacon Croaker's wool into smooth, even threads, but her heart ached as she prayed for her boy, and often, when in the still watches of the night Polly [124] kept her vigils with pain, she heard her cry softly:—

'Lemuel, Lemuel, oh! how could you, how could you do it?'

Her uncle's family were living abroad now, and it was from Paris that Belle wrote, announcing her engagement to Reginald Gordon.

'Just imagine, Paul,' the letter went on, 'I, of all possible people, a missionary's wife! But the fact of the matter is, my precious saint, your splendid, consecrated life made me tingle with shame to my finger tips when I thought of my aimless existence, and when I remembered how you took up your cross and followed your Master to Sleepy Hollow, there seemed to be no reason why I should not follow Him to Africa. If it will comfort you, I want you to know that you have been the guiding star which has led me [125] out of the sloth of my selfishness into active work for the King.'

The years slipped by peacefully after that. Her father grew daily more childish, and needed more constant watching, but she found time to read to Polly many a snatch from her favourite authors, and Tryphosa's Bible lay always open near her hand.

At last the day came when, in the full noontide, her father had called to her in his weak voice, 'It's gettin' dark, Pawliney, and Lemuel's not come home.'

And she had answered with her brave, sweet faith, 'Not yet, father, but he'll come by-and-by. God knows.'

'Yes, God knows,' said the old man with a peaceful smile, 'I think I'll go to sleep now, I'm very tired. You've been a good girl, Pawliney; a good girl. God bless you, my dear.'

[126] When the evening came Pauline laid her hand softly on the wrinkled brow, from which the shadows had forever lifted. 'Dear old father,' she whispered, 'how little I thought, when I wished you and I could leave Sleepy Hollow, that you would be the first one to go away!'

'You ought always to dress in silk, Pauline, instead of calico. I wish you could,' and Polly's eyes rested on her with a world of love in their depths.

Pauline laughed as she kissed her.

'You silly child! Don't you know that cotton grows, and silk has to be spun, which makes it costly? and cotton is content to be washed in spring water, while silk has to be bathed in tea. Can you spare me for a whole afternoon do you think, if I leave Carlyle and Whittier by your pillow?'

[127] 'Where are you going?'

'Well, I want to take some apple custard to that poor Dan who fell from the haymow, and I must go and see how Susan's children are getting through the measles. Then old Mrs Croaker wants to be sung to, and the widow Larkin wants to be read to, and Matilda Jones is "jest pinin' fer a talk."' She laughed merrily.

'I never saw anyone get so much into their lives,' said Polly wistfully. 'I am so useless.'

'You blessed child!' cried Pauline, with the tears in her eyes; 'you are our Angel of Patience. Don't ever call yourself useless, dear, you are the centre of gravity for Stephen and me.'

When the twilight fell she sat in her favourite position near the open door, looking up at the rose-tinted clouds, as she made Polly laugh with merry descriptions of her different visits.

[128] Suddenly she grew still, for a sun-browned, bearded man had crossed the threshold, and thrown a paper into her lap, saying huskily: —

'There's the mortgage, Pauline, to make a bonfire of. I've come home to stay.'

Before he had finished, her arms were around his neck, and Polly heard her cry softly, with the break of a great gladness in her voice: —

'Lemuel! Why, Lemuel!'

Back to contents

[129] *Chapter XI*

Pure Gold

Richard Everidge sat in his handsome library one evening in early summer, reading a letter from his only child, Muriel, the joy of his heart: —

> 'My Dearest Papa, — We are stopping now in the quaintest little place, a veritable Sleepy Hollow, like its name, where Rip Van Winkle might have snoozed away for centuries without fear of being disturbed.

> 'As I advised you in my last, we were on our way to Farningham, when something went wrong with the engine, and we had to stop here for repairs, [130] and mamma was so charmed with this

little village that she decided to stay awhile; she says it seems to suit her better than any place she has seen; poor mamma, I wish I could find some place where she would be satisfied. To me all the world seems so beautiful, but she says no one knows how to sympathise with her peculiar organisation.

'That was Saturday. On Sunday morning I went to the little church, mamma was too tired, and now comes the best part of the story. I was looking round watching the different families, all in their Sunday best, coming in and getting seated, when suddenly a woman's voice began to lead the little choir. I looked up with a start. She was tall and slender; and as she stood with lifted head singing her heart out, I don't think I ever saw such a splendid carriage, even at the President's [131] reception in Washington. She looked like a princess among the plain farmer folk; for a crown she had a mass of lovely soft white hair, and the sweetest, clearest eyes I ever saw. When she was singing "Coronation" (which was quite appropriate for a princess) it seemed as if she would lift the whole congregation up to God.

'After the service I could not help watching her for a minute, for, as you will have imagined ere this, my silly heart went out to her at once. She was the centre of a group; every one seemed to have something to say to her, and she was so nice with them all, kissing the children, and having a bright smile and word for some of the most uninteresting women and stupid-looking boys I ever saw. Just as I was going out of the door I felt a soft touch upon my arm, [132] and turned to find her beside me. I am free to confess I never received such a welcome to any church before.

'When I gave her my name she looked puzzled for a minute.

'"Everidge," she repeated. "It is, it must be; she would be just about your age. I believe you are the little Muriel that my cousin Belle used to write about. You must come home with me at once: your father was my dear friend in the long ago."

'And so here we are, ensconced with my princess. She has a wonderful way with her, for mamma came without making the slightest objection, and seems happier than I have seen her for months.

'There are just four in the family, besides Martha Spriggs, the funny old girl. My princess, and her two stepbrothers, Stephen and Lemuel, and Polly, [133] who has been a sufferer from spinal trouble all her life.

'It is the quaintest old house, with low, small rooms, except on the east side, where Captain Lemuel has added two large rooms with the loveliest bay windows, which are always full of flowers and sunshine. I think the neighbours are horrified that they use them for common. You know country people always keep their best parlours done up in must and green paper; but the princess says, "Nothing is too good for Polly and the boys!" They just idolize her, and I fancy they have good reason to, for, as Stephen said, in his queer, blunt way, "she comes as near to an angel as any mortal ever will." Captain Lemuel has been all over the world, and is very interesting. Mamma is so amused over his stories. Stephen is blunt, but I shouldn't be afraid to trust him with every [134] cent I owned, and Polly is just a bundle of sweetness and patience. I wish you could see how gentle these great, strong men are with her: Stephen won't let any one but himself carry her to bed, and

Lemuel is always ready to push her about in her wheel chair, and talk nonsense to her till she laughs and cries together.

'And the princess! She is just everything to everybody. I cannot fancy what the house would be without her. I only hope she won't die before Polly, for I'm sure it would kill her. She never takes her eyes off her when she is in the room, and when I teased her a little about it her eyes filled, and she cried softly:—

'"It's little wonder if I do love her, after thirty years of such nursing as no one even dreamed of." It made me almost wish to be sick myself.

'She has such a merry, tender way with [135] her. I do not wonder Lemuel says they don't mind rainy weather since Pauline makes sunshine to order. And she is the busiest creature! I believe she carries the whole of Sleepy Hollow on her heart and shoulders. She seems to have all the destitute and afflicted under her wing, and dispenses beef-tea and Bible promises with the same liberal hand.

'Oh! Papa, I am so glad we were detained at Sleepy Hollow, for at last I have found what I have been looking for—an absolutely Christ-like life. Your own little daughter, Muriel.'

Richard Everidge remained deep in thought for a long time after he had kissed the large, girlish signature; then he drew a sheet of paper towards him, and wrote, in his clear, bold hand:—

[136] 'My Darling Muriel,—I knew your princess, as she says, in "the long ago," and she is, as you have found her, pure gold.

'Make the most of your visit, for, next to your Bible, she is the best teacher you could have. Your loving 'Father.'

The days lengthened into weeks and the Everidges were still at the Farm.

'Why should you go?' Pauline said, in her cheery, unanswerable way, when they spoke of leaving: 'it does us good to have you, and it does you good to be here,' and Muriel and her mother were content.

'Princess,' said the girl one day, as she watched her moving lightly about the kitchen, 'I envy you your altitude.'

Pauline laughed merrily.

'You dear child! Every one gets up the mountain if they keep on climbing.'

[137] 'But I have not an atom of perseverance,' sighed Muriel. 'Christianity seems such a tremendous undertaking to me.'

'Let me give you what was to me the beginning of all Gospels: "The kingdom of heaven is just as near us as our work is, for the gate of heaven for each soul lies in the endeavour to do that work perfectly."'

'But, princess, you are such a royal creature. It seems such a waste for you to be buried here.'

'The King never wastes, little one. If we have the angel aim and standard, we can consecrate the smallest acts. Don't you know that "he who aims for perfectness in a trifle, is trying to do that trifle holily?"'

'You dear princess! You make me think of one of Murillo's pictures in the Louvre, which we saw when we were [138] abroad last year. It is the interior of a convent kitchen, and instead of mortals in old dresses doing the work, there are beautiful white-winged angels. One puts the kettle on the fire, and one is lifting up a pail of water, and one is at the kitchen dresser reaching up for plates.'

Pauline smiled.

'That is it exactly. How can anything we do be common when we remember our inheritance? You call me Princess, out of love, little one, but I am a princess in reality, for my Father is a King. Let me give you a good word which your father gave me long ago. "If you cannot realize your Ideal, you can at least idealize your Real." I have been trying to do it ever since.'

'That is just like papa,' said Muriel, with a proud smile. 'He says you are "pure gold," princess.'

[139] 'Did Rich—did your father say that?' cried Pauline, and Muriel looked up to see a soft flush in her face, while her eyes shone. 'The King's daughter is all glorious within,' she repeated slowly, 'her clothing is of wrought gold.' Then she chanted in her clear, triumphant voice: —

> '"They have clean robes,
> White robes;
> White robes are waiting for me!"

'Ah! little one, "the court dress of heaven differs somewhat from that of earth."'

'But, princess,' said Muriel wistfully, 'farm work and cooking and washing dishes over and over—it seems such drudgery.'

A great light broke over her face, and she cried in a low, exultant tone: —

'"Blessed be Drudgery!" Christ bore [140] it for thirty years, why should I mind for forty-nine? I have only to wait a little now for the "fulness of joy" and "pleasures for evermore."'

Muriel threw her arms about her and kissed her softly.

'Then our princess will be at home,' she whispered, 'in the Palace of the King.'

TURNBULL AND SPEARS, PRINTERS, EDINBURGH.